Robot Boy and Frog Girl!

T0337047

Written by Barbara MacKay
Illustrated by Anna Hancock

Collins

Who and what is in this story?

Listen and say 🎧

Jo

Mim

frog

Download the audio at www.collins.co.uk/839809

Tom

robot

5

7

The football is in the tree.

10

Jo jumps. She is in the flowers!

Mim the cat runs and jumps!

13

Tom and Jo play a game.

Do not look,
Robot boy!

Where is Jo?

I see Frog girl!

Where is Tom?

Frog girl sees Robot boy!

You are funny, Tom!

19

Pop!

Thank you, Frog girl!

We are Frog girl and Robot boy!

21

Picture dictionary

Listen and repeat 🎧③

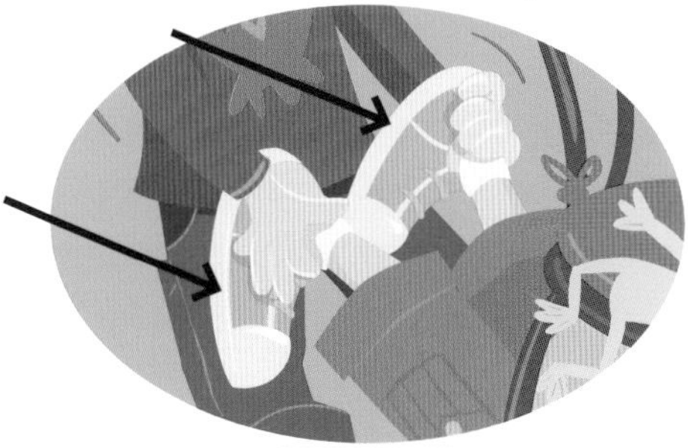

feet

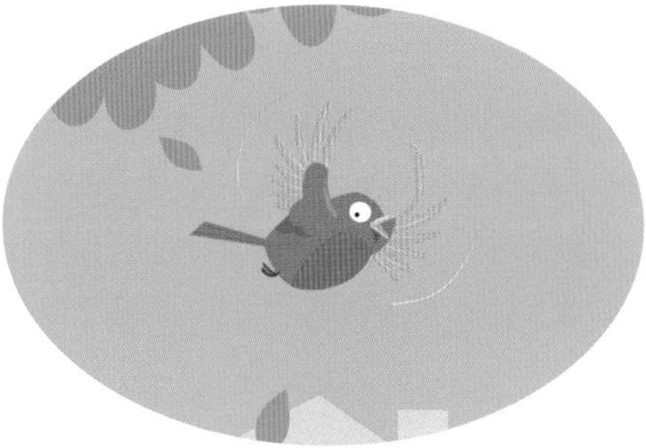

fly

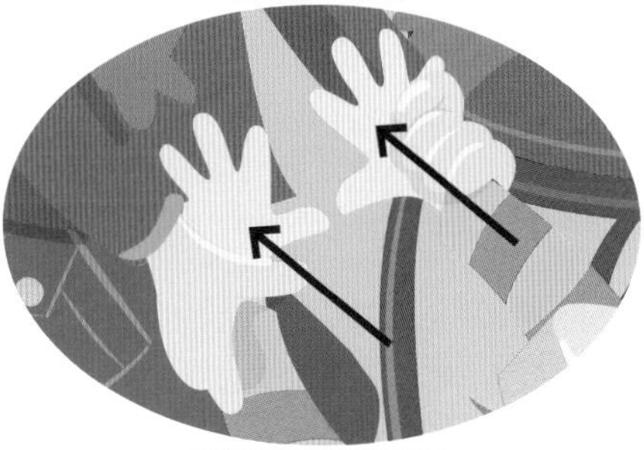

hands

jump

kick

run

1 Look and order the story

2 Listen and say

Collins

Published by Collins
An imprint of HarperCollins*Publishers*
Westerhill Road
Bishopbriggs
Glasgow
G64 2QT

HarperCollins*Publishers*
1st Floor, Watermarque Building
Ringsend Road
Dublin 4
Ireland

William Collins' dream of knowledge for all began with the publication of his first book in 1819.

A self-educated mill worker, he not only enriched millions of lives, but also founded a flourishing publishing house. Today, staying true to this spirit, Collins books are packed with inspiration, innovation and practical expertise. They place you at the centre of a world of possibility and give you exactly what you need to explore it.

© HarperCollins*Publishers* Limited 2020

10 9 8 7 6 5 4 3 2

ISBN 978-0-00-839809-5

Collins® and COBUILD® are registered trademarks of HarperCollins*Publishers* Limited

www.collins.co.uk/elt

Author: Barbara MacKay
Illustrator: Anna Hancock (Beehive)
Series editor: Rebecca Adlard
Commissioning editor: Zoë Clarke
Publishing manager: Lisa Todd
Product managers: Jennifer Hall and Caroline Green
In-house editor: Alma Puts Keren
Project manager: Emily Hooton
Editor: Emma Wilkinson
Proofreaders: Natalie Murray and Michael Lamb
Cover designer: Kevin Robbins
Typesetter: 2Hoots Publishing Services Ltd
Audio produced by id audio, London
Reading guide author: Emma Wilkinson
Production controller: Rachel Weaver
Printed and bound by: GPS Group, Slovenia

British Library Cataloguing in Publication Data

A catalogue record for this publication is available from the British Library.

Download the audio for this book and a reading guide for parents and teachers at www.collins.co.uk/839809